GREEK GODS and Goddesses
I AM HERA!

WRITTEN BY
THOMAS KINGSLEY TROUPE

ILLUSTRATED BY
FELISHIA HENDITIRTO

TABLE OF CONTENTS

A Mermaid Book
SEAHORSE
PUBLISHING

Good day, mortal one!
I trust you have heard
of me? I'm the ancient
Greek goddess of women,
childbirth, and marriage.

I'm also the wife of Zeus,
king of all gods on Mount
Olympus. That makes
me queen, and don't you
forget it! All know me, and
I require no introduction. I
am Hera!

As a goddess, I have many powers. I control how long or short the birth of a child will be. I decide if a marriage shall succeed or fail. And, due to my love of animals, I can shapeshift into any creature.

As you might imagine, I've had quite an interesting life. Let me tell you my story.

3

My life wasn't simple from the start, and it became even more difficult.

My father was the god of time, Cronus. He ruled over all the gods atop Mount Olympus. Cronus knew about a prophecy that said one of his children would overthrow him and take his power. And he didn't like that idea at all!

So whenever my mother, Rhea, gave birth, Cronus took the baby and swallowed it. Shortly after I was born, Cronus gobbled me up. For a long time, I sat in my father's stomach with my sisters and brothers.

My mother didn't like seeing all her kids disappear, so she made a plan. When my baby brother was born, she hid him away. She wrapped a stone in blankets and gave it to Cronus. He quickly swallowed the stone, thinking it was his son.

That baby brother was none other than Zeus. Hidden away from Cronus, he grew tall and strong. When Zeus was old enough, he gave a cup of poison to Father. Cronus drank it and became sick.

All it took was a little barfing for my sisters, brothers, and I to be freed from Dad's gut.

We were all grown up and released from our stomach prison. Cronus was not happy with us. We were not very happy with him, either! A war for power began.

Father called his Titans, the old gods. They helped him fight us in a battle that lasted ten years. My sisters, brothers, and I were victorious. We became the rulers of Mount Olympus.

My siblings and I divided up the world. My brother Zeus became god of the air and sky. Poseidon commanded the seas. Poor Hades got stuck being king of the underworld. Hestia became the goddess of the hearth and home, and Demeter was goddess of the harvest.

Me? I would oversee the lives of mortal women. I would watch over the birth of their children. It was also my job to guide human marriages. In my spare time, I loved to be among animals.

I found out that my brother Zeus had fallen in love with me. I told him I wasn't interested, but unfortunately Zeus is not the kind of god who takes "no" for an answer.

Zeus knew of my love for animals. One cold and stormy night, I heard a flutter outside. When I opened my window, I saw a cuckoo bird, wet and miserable from the rain. Of course, I brought the poor dear inside and held it close to warm it up.

That "cuckoo" turned out to be Zeus! He had turned himself into the bird to trick me. I was completely ashamed. Zeus demanded that I marry him or else he'd tell everyone that I'd been fooled.

Before I knew it, I was married to Zeus. Together we became king and queen of the gods, ruling from our palace high on Mount Olympus.

But I never forgot that Zeus had tricked me. I knew that someday I would have my revenge.

Zeus was NOT a good husband. It turns out that he loved many others besides me. One was a mortal woman named Semele. She had sacrificed a bull on the altar of Zeus. Seeing this, Zeus immediately fell in love with her.

Zeus made himself into a human so that he could be with Semele. The two had a secret romance, and soon Semele became pregnant.

I was enraged at my husband. I disguised myself as a mortal woman and befriended Semele. In time, Semele told me she was in love with a god. I pretended I didn't believe her and asked her to prove it.

Zeus had promised Semele that he would grant any wish she had. The next time Zeus visited, Semele decided to prove to me who the man really was. She asked Zeus to show his true godly form.

Unable to break his promise to Semele, Zeus revealed his true self. But mortals aren't allowed to see gods. As soon as she glimpsed the god Zeus, Semele burst into flames and died. Zeus did manage to save the unborn baby, who became the god Dionysus.

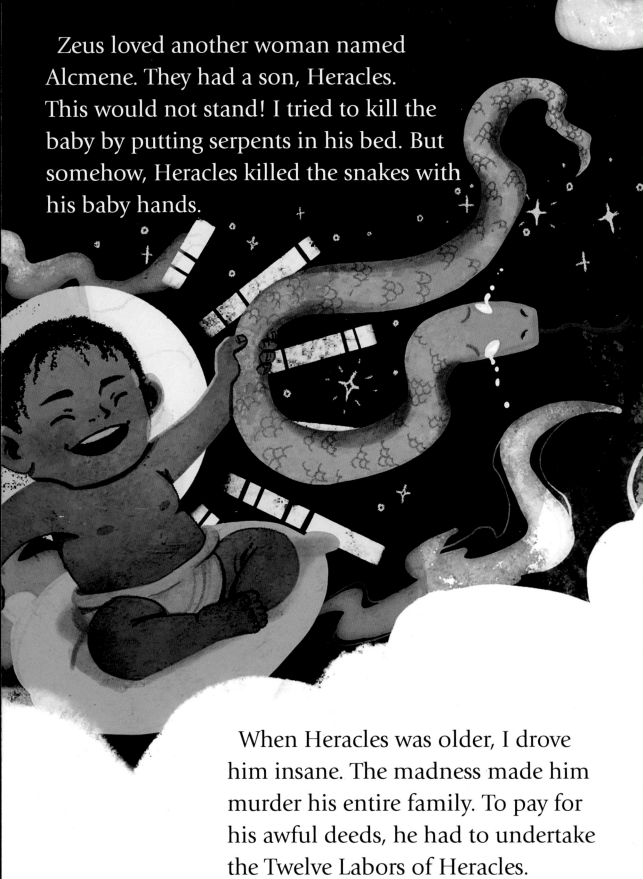

Zeus loved another woman named Alcmene. They had a son, Heracles. This would not stand! I tried to kill the baby by putting serpents in his bed. But somehow, Heracles killed the snakes with his baby hands.

When Heracles was older, I drove him insane. The madness made him murder his entire family. To pay for his awful deeds, he had to undertake the Twelve Labors of Heracles.

They were VERY hard tasks to complete. Heracles had to slay and capture many monsters. One was a nine-headed hydra. In a single day, he had to clean the stables of King Augeas where a thousand cows lived. Yuck! Despite it all, Heracles finished his tasks and became a well-known hero.

I'm not proud of all the decisions I've made, but I'm always proud of my kids!

My son Ares, the god of war, remained on Mount Olympus as one of the twelve supreme gods.

My daughter Hebe grew up to be the beautiful goddess of youth. She did marry that hero Heracles, but I forgave her for it.

My son Hephaestus became the god of blacksmiths, metalworking, and fire. He stayed very busy making swords, helmets, and armor for all the gods.

There are many other stories to tell, but I feel I have said enough. At least you know that I did get my revenge on that lousy Zeus.

Think of me, young mortal, when you attend a wedding or see a newborn baby. Know that I am watching over.

Remember my power! I am the queen. I am HERA!

What Is Greek Mythology?

Greek mythology is a collection of epic stories about gods, goddesses, heroes, strange creatures, and the origins of the civilization of ancient Greece. For hundreds of years before they were first written down, the stories were told and retold orally by the ancient Greeks. The tales were passed down over generations and are still known today as myths and legends.

Questions for Discussion

1. Would you say Hera was a good goddess or a bad goddess? What are some things she did that were good? What did she do that was bad? What was out of her control?

2. How did Zeus trick Hera? How did his trick influence the rest of Hera's life and her relationships with others?

3. What fact about Hera is your favorite? Explain why.

Writing Activity

Choose part of Hera's story to rewrite. Imagine that she is not fooled by Zeus, that she becomes Semele's real friend, that she falls in love with Heracles, or something else. Write the new story and explain how it changes Hera's life. Does it make her happier and less focused on revenge?

About the Author

Thomas Kingsley Troupe is the author of over 200 books for young readers. When he's not writing, he enjoys reading, playing video games, and investigating haunted places with the Twin Cities Paranormal Society. Otherwise, he's probably taking a nap or something. Thomas lives in Woodbury, Minnesota, with his two sons.

About the Illustrator

Felishia Henditirto was born in Bandung, Indonesia, and has been fascinated by art and stories since she was a child. When everybody else in class was busy taking notes, she was stuck in her own world, drawing. She always has a thirst for magic and tries to find it in everything she does, especially in reading! If she is not working, you can find her visiting far, faraway places in the pages of a book.

Written by: Thomas Kingsley Troupe
Illustrated by: Felishia Henditirto
Design by: Under the Oaks Media
Series Development: James Earley
Editor: Kim Thompson

Library of Congress PCN Data
I Am Hera! / Thomas Kingsley Troupe
Greek Gods and Goddesses
ISBN 979-8-8873-5935-9 (hard cover)
ISBN 979-8-8873-5974-8 (paperback)
ISBN 979-8-8904-2033-6 (EPUB)
ISBN 979-8-8904-2092-3 (eBook)
Library of Congress Control Number: 2023912371

Printed in the United States of America.

Seahorse Publishing Company
www.seahorsepub.com

Published in the United States
Seahorse Publishing
PO Box 771325
Coral Springs, FL 33077

SEAHORSE PUBLISHING